W9-CAT-633

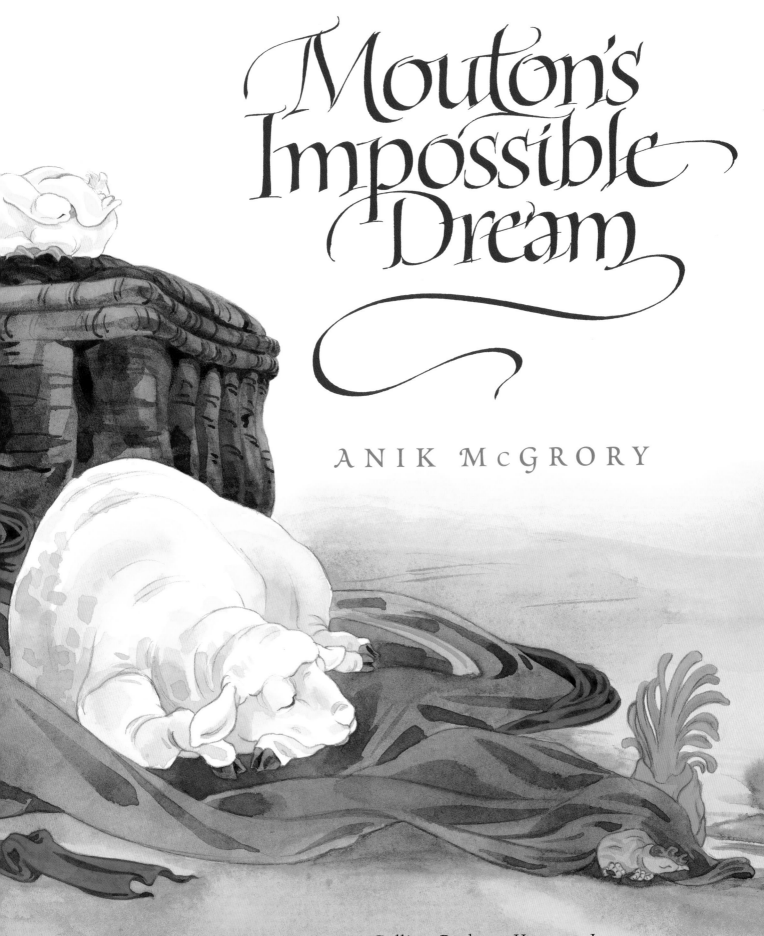

Mouton's Impossible Dream

ANIK McGRORY

Gulliver Books • Harcourt, Inc.

San Diego   New York   London

la pompe
à feu

Library of Congress Cataloging-in-Publication Data
McGrory, Anik.
Mouton's impossible dream/Anik McGrory.
p   cm.
"Gulliver Books."
Summary: Mouton the sheep is fascinated
by the thought of flying, and she gets her wish
when she is sent up in the Montgolfier brothers'
hot air balloon in 1783.
[1. Sheep—Fiction.   2. Hot air balloons—Fiction.
3. Balloon ascensions—Fiction.
4. Montgolfier, Jacques-Etienne, 1745–1799—Fiction.
5. Montgolfier, Joseph-Michel, 1740–1810—Fiction.]
I. Title.
PZ7.M173Mo   2000   98-47275
ISBN 0-15-202195-7

First edition
A C E F D B
Printed in Hong Kong

The illustrations in this book were done in watercolors
on Fabriano Artistico watercolor paper.
The display type was hand-lettered by John Stevens.
The text type was set in Deepdene.
Color separations by Bright Arts Ltd., Hong Kong
Printed by South China Printing Company, Ltd., Hong Kong
This book was printed on totally chlorine-free
Nymolla Matte Art paper.
Production supervision by Stanley Redfern
Designed by Lydia D'moch

Once there was a sheep who dreamed the impossible. Her name was Mouton, and she lived on a farm in southern France. Every day on her way to the field to graze, she stopped, mesmerized by the curious drawings tacked on the barn walls by the Brothers who owned the farm.

"Someday I'm going to fly," she whispered.

With a rustle and a flop, Canard the duck tumbled
down to the ground. "I can teach you to fly," he quacked,
untangling his feet.

Mouton's eyes glistened.

Cocorico the rooster scratched nearby. "Flying is silliness,"
he clucked. "And anyway, sheep are not made to *fly*."

From that day on, Mouton was very busy.
During the days she studied the Brothers and
their flying machines.

In the evenings she studied Canard
and his wings and feathers.

But when the time came for Mouton's first flight, she just wasn't ready.

Still, that night she dreamed about flying.

The next morning Mouton was startled awake by the sound of the Brothers packing for a journey. She watched helplessly as they tucked their precious drawings away in their wagon, along with boxes and baskets, rolls of rope, heaps of linen, and mammoth sheets of paper. They even packed Cocorico.

"Where are they taking Cocorico?" quacked Canard.

"Where are they taking my drawings?" bleated Mouton.

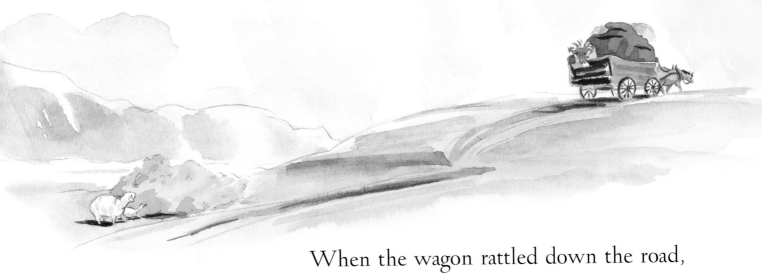

When the wagon rattled down the road,
Canard and Mouton followed close behind,
carefully keeping out of sight.

Just before sunset Cocorico fell off the wagon.
"Can you take me home now?" he asked, relieved
to be rescued. But Mouton had other ideas.

Mouton, Canard, and Cocorico followed
the wagon past villages and through cities.
After a very long time, they arrived at a palace
that glowed like the sun. There a flock of
people were gathering around the wagon.

Mouton could see one of the Brothers unpacking the flying machine. Nearby a little boy shouted, "If people can fly, we can do anything!"

Mouton pushed to get closer.

"That thing will never get off the ground," said an innkeeper.

"And surely the air way up in the sky isn't safe to breathe," added a doctor.

Mouton brushed past them. At the edge
of the crowd, she spotted an empty basket.
With Canard and Cocorico, she slipped inside
to wait and watch unseen.

Just as the animals settled in, they heard the people cheer. Cocorico stretched his neck and scrambled for a better look. "It's the king and queen!" he squealed, forgetting to hide.

The people bowed down to the ground.

Looking rather skeptical, the king inquired about the Brothers' invention. As one of the Brothers described how their machine would soar to the skies, the queen smiled with delight. "But what are the animals for?" she asked.

Il e**
mign

Everyone looked confused. Then one of the Brothers smiled. "They'll test the balloon for us!" he said. "If the animals can fly, we'll know it's safe!"

"Flying is *not* safe," screeched Cocorico as he struggled to escape. But no one heeded his warning.

From inside the basket, the animals heard fluttering and flumping. And then everything went still. Mouton waited and listened. Suddenly the basket jumped. Mouton's heart leaped. But only a second later, the basket bumped back to the ground.

Canard looked at Mouton. "I'm sorry, Mouton," he said when he saw her face, "but maybe Cocorico was right—maybe sheep just aren't made to fly."

Just then the basket jumped again.
This time it didn't bump back to the
ground. It went up and up. The crowd
gasped.

Mouton squeezed her head out and peered
down at the ground. She was flying!

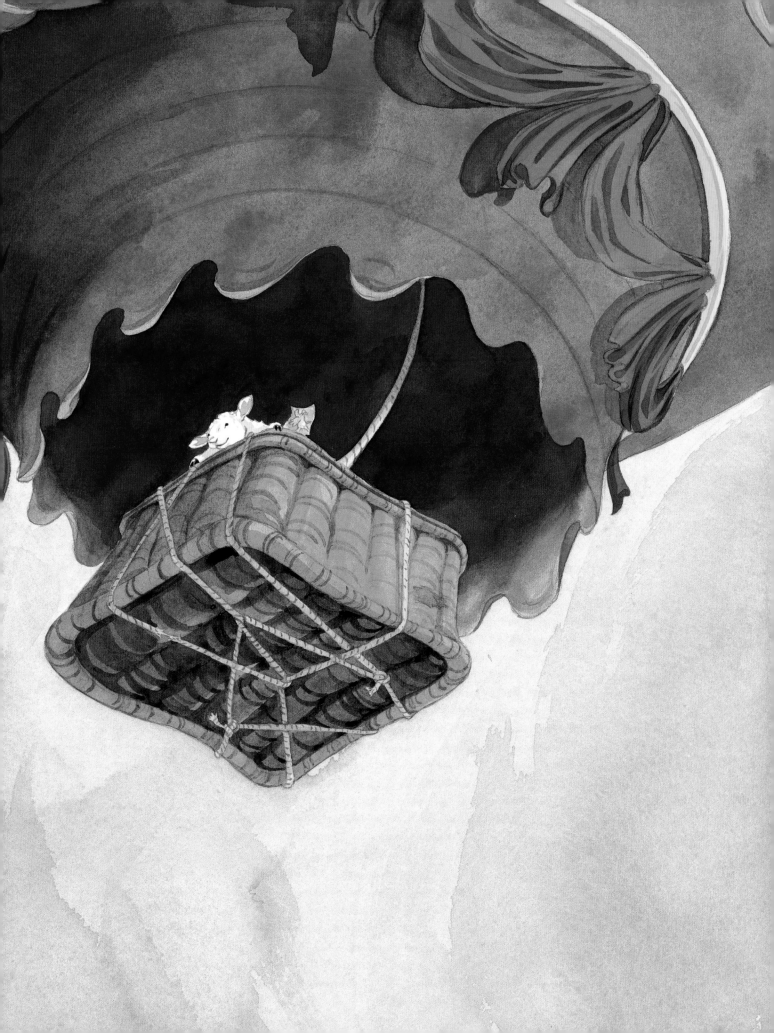

Canard was astounded. Without flapping their wings, he, Mouton, and Cocorico were moving across the sky like a cloud.

Cocorico fought to get loose but quickly changed his mind when he saw the world drop from under them.

BEEEKAAAAWD

The animals drifted over fields and forests, gliding and hovering and floating until at last the machine slowly began settling back to earth.

And then *thud*. Their journey was over.

Cocorico crowed the happiest crow of his life. He had flown, but he was alive! "Mouton, did you see? We were soaring!"

Mouton just gazed up at the sky and whispered, "I was flying."

Canard smoothed his feathers and looked hard at Cocorico. He thought Cocorico didn't *like* flying.

Mouton, Canard, and Cocorico were royally rewarded for their bravery. The queen was so impressed with their flight that she invited them all to live at the palace.

There Canard spent his days giving lessons to Cocorico, who found that he actually enjoyed flying—and didn't even mind an occasional crash.

Mouton became a favorite with the royal family. Having fulfilled her greatest desire, she lived the rest of her life with her feet on the ground and her dreams in the clouds.

Au revoir

Historical Notes

This story is not far from the truth. On September 19, 1783, a sheep, a duck, and a rooster flew in the world's first "passengered" hot-air balloon, which had been designed by Joseph and Etienne Montgolfier. The event took place at the palace of Versailles, outside Paris, and the royal family attended the launch. One hundred thirty thousand spectators witnessed the event. The balloon, made from cloth and paper, sailed for eight minutes and flew about two miles.

The rooster damaged a wing during the flight. It is thought that he was kicked by the sheep. After the launch, the sheep was sent to live in Marie Antoinette's animal menagerie at Versailles. No one knows what happened to the rooster or the duck.

The animals' balloon ride paved the way for human flight. Because the animals survived the flight, the Montgolfiers knew that the air in the sky was safe to breathe. On November 21 of the same year, the Montgolfier brothers launched the world's first manned free-flying balloon. The balloon flew for twenty-five minutes and traveled five miles.

The sheep, the duck, and the rooster set a precedent for experimental flights of other animals. They also set off a craze of balloon flying that spread throughout Europe and America.